For Donna

First edition for the United States, Canada and the Philippines
published 1988 by Barron's Educational Series

First published 1988 by Piccadilly Press Ltd., London, England

Text and illustrations © Richard Fowler, 1988

All inquiries should be addressed to:
Barron's Educational Series, Inc.
250 Wireless Boulevard
Hauppauge, New York 11788

Library of Congress Catalog Card No. 88-6287

International Standard Book No. 0-8120-5920-4

Library of Congress Cataloging-in-Publication Data

Fowler, Richard. 1944-
Cat's car/ Richard Fowler.--1st ad.
p.   ca.
Summary: Cat's automobile trip to the beach is interrupted
when his animal friends ask for a lift.
ISBN 0-8120-5920-4
[1. Animal--Fiction.   2. Automobiles--Fiction.]   I. Title.
PZ8.F8296Cau   1988   88-6287
CIP
AC

[E]--dc19

Printed in Great Britain

890 9697 987654321

Cat's Car

Richard Fowler

BARRON'S
New York · Toronto

Early one summer morning,
Cat jumped into his old car
and set off on a drive to the beach.

"What a lovely day to get away from it all,"
thought Cat as he drove along
in the warm sunshine.

Around a bend in the road
Cat saw Bear waving for him to stop.

"Bother!" said Cat. "I wonder what Bear wants."

"I've run out of honey," said Bear.
"Be a good Cat and give me a lift to the farm."

"Oh, all right," sighed Cat. "Jump in!"

At the farm Bear went off in search of honey. Cat was about to go when Goat asked him to deliver a shopping list to Tiger.

"I'd take it myself," said Goat, "but I'd probably eat it on the way!"

Cat popped the list into Tiger's letter box.
He soon came across Penguin sitting on a block
of ice! Cat stopped the car.

"I must get this ice home before it melts,"
said Penguin, "or else my fish will go bad."
"Jump in!" said Cat.
They got to Penguin's house in time to
save the fish, but not before Cat's car
was soaked!

"Now for the beach," said Cat.
He was driving through some woods
when there was a loud SNAP, then a SPLASH!
A branch of a tree fell into the back seat
of Cat's car.

Cat was amazed to find Monkey sitting among the leaves.

"It's my lucky day," said Monkey.

"It's not turning out to be mine," grumbled Cat.

"I'm trying to get to the beach!"

"Can I come with you?" asked Monkey.

"I suppose so," said Cat. "Jump in!"

"I already have," giggled Monkey.

Suddenly, Rabbit hopped out in front
of the car. Cat stopped just in time!

"Where are you going in such a hurry?" asked Cat.

"I'm trying to get to the beach,"
exclaimed a frightened Rabbit.

"So are we," said Cat. "Hop in!"

A mile down the road Monkey yelled:
"Look, there's Tiger. Do stop."
Tiger was holding two large shopping bags,
and looked rather cross.

"I've just missed the bus," growled Tiger. "I was late because that silly Goat put my shopping list in next-door's letter box!"

"Oh dear," mumbled Cat going red. "Would you like to join us?"

Tiger jumped into the car,
then he jumped out again!
Cat's car wouldn't start.

"Bother," cried Cat. "I've run out of gas
I've been driving around so much . . ."

"Some lift," growled Tiger as he, Monkey
and Rabbit started to push.

They came to an intersection.

"Look, there's a sign to the beach," said Tiger.

"There's another one," said Monkey.

"Which way is the quickest?" asked Cat.

None of them knew.

"We could spin a carrot," suggested Rabbit.

"Good idea," said the others.

They spun the carrot on the car's hood.

When it stopped it pointed to the right.

"Let's go," they cried.

Soon the sea came into view.

"Don't push so hard," yelled Cat.

"We're not," cried the others,
hanging on to the back.

"This must be the quick way," shouted Cat.
The little car sped down the hill,
and landed on the beach . . .

CRASH!

. . . next to Bear, Goat, and Penguin,
who were sitting on the sand.
Tiger's shopping bags burst open,
and they were all showered with food and drinks!
"Lunch is now being served," chuckled Bear,
as he grabbed a honey sandwich.

They all had a great day on the beach,
and when it was time to go,
they took turns pushing Cat's car
all the way home!